Margaret's Unicorn

Margaret's Unicorn

by Briony May Smith

Schwartz & Wade Books • New York

My whole world changed when we moved to a faraway place, to a cottage in the mountains, to be near Grandma.

Everything smelled different and strange, and the house was full of empty spaces.

That first afternoon, Dad said, "Margaret, why don't you
go exploring? By the time you come back, your new room will
look just like your old room. I promise."

Mom put hot chocolate in a thermos. "Be careful not to go
farther than the big stone," she said, and gave me a kiss.

When I reached the big stone at the end of our garden,
I saw the sea spread out before me. A heavy fog was traveling
through the sky, and soon the water was covered in mist.

No, that wasn't mist; it was clouds. No, they weren't
clouds; they were white horses. No, not horses—*unicorns!*

They were leaping into the air, swept up by the wind.
And then, in a blink, they were gone.

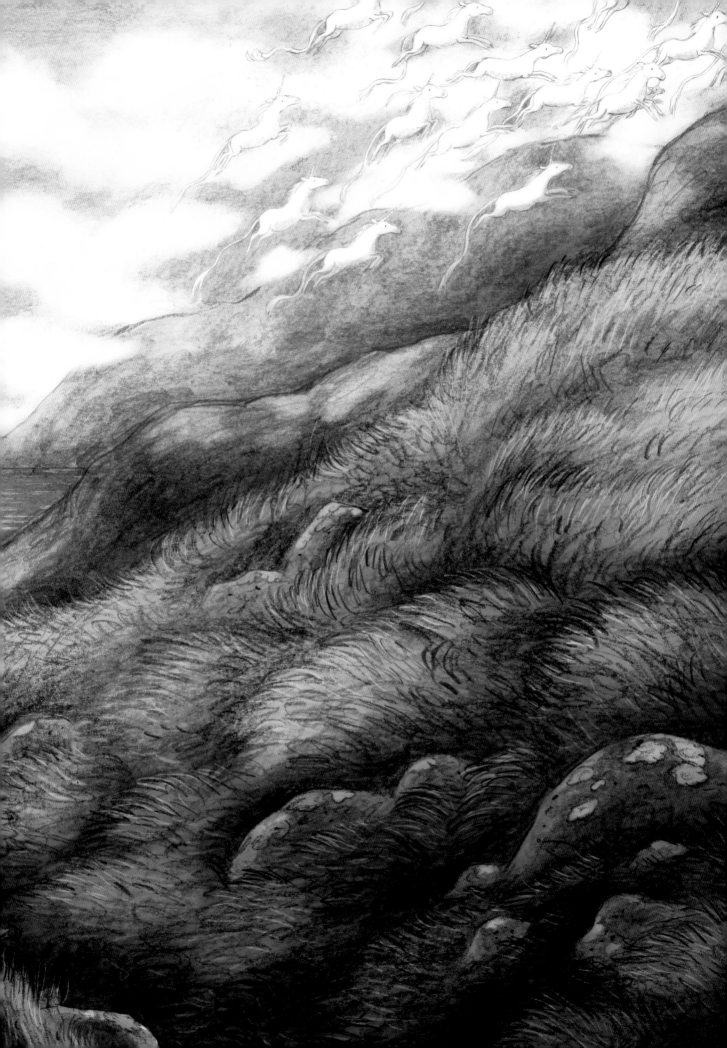

I started to run back to tell Mom and Dad, when I heard a snuffling noise.

I tiptoed closer and closer . . . down a little dip, where
something silvery lay tangled in the weeds. "A baby!" I gasped.

Carefully I freed him, then wrapped him in my coat.

When I got home, Grandma was at the door. She'd come by to help us unpack.

"I didn't think there were any left," she said.

I told her all about the herd that had flown past me.

"When I was a girl," she said, smiling, "we would watch the unicorns fly off to Unicorn Island on the last summer wind."

Grandma told me everything she knew about unicorns. "They only eat flowers, but there aren't enough here to feed them all year round. Every spring I would wait for them to come back to eat the young heather and thistles that grow across the mountains."

I looked out our cottage window. There were hardly any flowers to be seen. "What will we feed him?" I asked.

Grandma thought for a moment. "Let's go!" she said.
We jumped into the car and headed into town.

At a small shop, we bought bunches
of flowers for my little unicorn.

When we got home, we fed him.

"What do unicorns drink?" I asked Grandma.

"Water that has been touched by moonlight," she explained. "It's what makes their horns glow in the dark. It's what gives them their magic."

I stroked my unicorn's mane, and Grandma and I fished pillows
out of the moving boxes to make him a cozy nest near my bed.

After Mom and Dad had finished unloading the boxes, they came in to
find us with my little unicorn. Mom knelt beside him and he nuzzled her hand.

That night, Dad and I pulled on our boots and headed out to the hills.

As soon as the moon touched the stream, we filled buckets with water and carried them home.

The water glowed in our dark garage.
My unicorn drank as we watched him, amazed.

When I went to sleep, I let the little unicorn climb
into bed with me, and I stroked his speckled coat.
My unicorn whimpered. I was so excited to have found
him, I'd forgotten how scared he must be!
"It's okay," I whispered. "Spring will be back in no time."

The next day, my unicorn and I went for a walk. We crunched
through the leaves and caught them as they floated down from the trees.
I picked up a horse chestnut, opened it carefully, and touched its soft
inside, which felt like a little fairy fur coat.

That evening we watched the stars come out before heading to bed. They seemed so much brighter here than in our old town.

By the time all the trees were bare, my little unicorn had grown
comfortable in our cottage. One of our favorite things to do was
go to the beach and chase the waves. The white foam looked like
unicorns, rolling and disappearing into the sandy shore.

Then we'd race home with cold fingers and toes—and hooves!

"A fire," I'd tell my unicorn, "is the best thing to cozy up to."

We'd curl up together and listen to the rain tap-tap-tap
on the window. "Isn't that the loveliest sound?" I'd say.

At Christmas, we decorated the tree,

and the house was filled with smells of our old home.

When it snowed for the first time, my unicorn was dazzled by it, and by how quiet everything became. We walked down the road and stomped on the frozen puddles.

Together we made a snow unicorn. Dad broke off an
icicle that hung from the roof, and we gave it a crystal horn.
I was missing our old home less and less.

The weather grew warmer, and I saw buds appear on the
trees and green shoots start to push up through the ground.

Yellow gorse and dandelion flowers started to bloom in the hills.
Soon, I knew, my unicorn's family would come back and he would leave.

When a unicorn is your friend, you wish spring would stay far away.

On the first day of spring, as we sat on the hill, the
unicorns floated down from the sky like snowflakes.

Slowly, one of them, with chocolate-brown
eyes and a soft pink nose, drew close.

My unicorn skipped toward her and leaned against her white
coat. He nuzzled her cheek. I knew this must be his mother.

It was time to say goodbye to my unicorn. "Please don't forget me," I whispered into a silky ear as I hugged him tightly.

Now spring has come and gone, and the days have grown longer.

I've made some new friends, but I do still miss my unicorn.

One day we went walking over the hills—Mom
and Dad and Grandma, my friend Abbie, and me.

As Abbie and I were searching for bugs in the tall grass,
something nudged my arm, and I turned in surprise.

It was my unicorn! He had grown
so much already and lost his baby coat.
When he raised his head, he was taller
than me. Wild and beautiful.

I plucked a sprig of heather from its stem and held out my palm. Cautiously, my unicorn ate it from my hand, watching me with his dark eyes. His ears flicked back and forth, listening to all around him. I wanted to reach out and touch him.

He took one more flower, and then he must have heard
something, or maybe I moved too quickly, because he turned
and galloped away in an instant. I scrambled a few paces after him
and watched him disappear into the mountains. He was gone.

I turned to Abbie, who looked on in amazement.
"That was an old friend," I said.

Mom called. It was time to head home, through the
heather and the thistles, to our cottage in the mountains.

The End

For Mum and Dad

All rights reserved. Published in the United States by Schwartz & Wade Books, an imprint of
Random House Children's Books, a division of Penguin Random House LLC, New York.
Schwartz & Wade Books and the colophon are trademarks of Penguin Random House LLC.
Visit us on the Web! rhcbooks.com
Educators and librarians, for a variety of teaching tools, visit us at RHTeachersLibrarians.com
Library of Congress Cataloging-in-Publication Data is available upon request.
ISBN 978-1-9848-9653-7 (trade) — ISBN 978-1-9848-9654-4 (lib. bdg.) — ISBN 978-1-9848-9655-1 (ebook)
The text of this book is set in 14-point Garamond Premier Pro.
The illustrations were rendered in mixed media.
MANUFACTURED IN CHINA
6 8 10 9 7 5
First Edition